LOOKING FOR HOME

Also by Eileen M. Berry

Roses on Baker Street
Haiku on Your Shoe
Buttercup Hill
Benjamin's Sling

LOOKING FOR HOME

Eileen M. Berry

Illustrated by
Maurie J. Manning

journeyforth®

Greenville, South Carolina

Library of Congress Cataloging-in-Publication Data

Berry, Eileen M., date–
   Looking for home / by Eileen M. Berry.
      p. cm.
   Summary: After living in the country, having to be quiet
and follow all the rules of their apartment complex is hard
for Micah and Liz, but when they befriend Grandma Jan, a
homesick neighbor, Micah is not sure he wants to move to a
house again.
   ISBN 1-59166-493-4 (perfect bound pbk. : alk. paper)
   [1. Moving, Household—Fiction. 2. Homesickness—
Fiction. 3. City and town life—Fiction. 4. Neighborliness—
Fiction.] I. Title.
   PZ7.B46168Loo 2005
   [Fic]—dc22

                                              2005024319

Design by Rita Golden
Composition by Michael Boone

Illustrations copyright © 2006 Maurie J. Manning
Text copyright © 2006 BJU Press
Greenville, South Carolina 29609
JourneyForth Books is a division of BJU Press.

Printed in the United States of America

ISBN 978-1-59166-493-2
eISBN 978-1-60682-994-3

15 14 13 12 11 10 9 8

In loving memory
of Nettie Berry and Emogene Lockridge,
my dear grandmothers
who are both safe at Home.

Contents

Chapter 1
Digging for Treasure

Geese are not my favorite birds. They are big and mean and noisy. And this one was asking for trouble. He was staring at me and hissing.

I raised my stick and edged closer. "Hand over the gold," I said. "Hand it over now, or I'll make you walk the plank!" Then I ran right at him.

Honk-honk! He waddled off, flapping his wings. I fell in the grass laughing.

"Micah!" Liz shouted at me. "Mom said not to chase the geese."

I sat up and looked back at our building. I found our apartment window—the one on the ground floor with the yellow curtains. Mom was not looking out.

I sighed. "I was just being a pirate." I stood up and threw my stick into the pond.

Before, when we lived in Michigan, we could chase things. But here in the city it's different. We have a pond behind our building, but we can't wade or fish in it. We have trees, but we can't climb them. We can't even put up a tire swing. Dad says the neighbors might not like that.

Liz was on her knees beneath a tree, all hunched down. I wandered over.

"What are you doing?" I asked.

She held up her toy shovel. "Digging for treasure. Want to help?"

Liz is two years older than me. She really knows how to come up with ideas. Good ones. I ran to our sandbox to get my shovel.

"Do you think pirates really buried treasure here?" I asked.

"I think there's a good chance," said Liz. "We're closer to the ocean here than we were in Michigan."

Finding treasure would make everything all right. That would make up for having to leave our house in the country. That would make up for moving here even though we have to be quieter indoors and can't chase things.

I started digging.

My shovel hit something hard. "I found something!" I said. "I think it's a treasure chest!"

"Be careful when you clear away the dirt," said Liz. "Old wood like that is all soft and squishy. You don't want to poke a hole in it."

Crack! The handle broke off my shovel.

Liz crawled over and peered into the hole I had started. "Micah," she said, "that's a tree root."

"Oh." I tossed the broken halves of my shovel down.

I looked over Liz's head, and something caught my eye. An old lady with white hair and a brown jacket was walking from the apartments down to the pond. "Look at that lady," I said.

Liz took a long look over her shoulder. "I think she's a pirate in disguise," she said. "Let's spy on her. Behind the tree—quick!"

We crouched down in the tree's shadow. The lady did not look our way at all. She stopped right at the edge of the pond and stood with her arms crossed.

"She knows where the treasure is," Liz whispered. "She's trying to think of a way to get it without anyone seeing."

"But we'll see!" I said.

Liz put her finger to her lips.

The lady walked slowly along the bank. "She's making a map in her head," said Liz. "See how she's looking at everything? She's going to go back inside and draw it. Then she's going to mark the treasure spot with a big red *X* . . ." Liz's voice trailed off.

The lady took something white out of her pocket. She dabbed at her eyes with it. Then she put it back. She tilted her head up to the sky and closed her eyes.

"What's she doing now?" I asked Liz.

Liz was quiet for a minute. "Thinking. Or maybe praying," said Liz.

"She's not a pirate, is she?"

Liz shook her head. "I don't think so." She watched for another moment. "But let's go say hi."

Chapter 2
Pilgrims Together

I think we scared the lady when we came running out from behind the tree. She kind of jumped and backed up a few steps.

"Hi," said Liz. "I'm Liz, and this is my brother Micah. Do you live here?"

The lady blinked a few times. Then she smiled. "Yes, I do. I just moved into Apartment 73. I'm Mrs. Janeski. It's kind of a mouthful. Juh-NES-key. Very nice to meet you." She held out her hand to Liz first and then to me. We both shook it.

"We live over there," said Liz, pointing to our window. "Where the yellow curtains are. We're not going to be in these apartments much longer. We're looking for a house."

"Oh. Have you moved here from far away?"

"We used to live in Michigan," said Liz, "in a big house in the country. But then our dad got a new job, and we came here."

Mrs. Janeski nodded. "I understand how that feels," she said. "I lived in the country all my life until now." She looked past us to watch a duck swimming across the water. "I sure do miss the country."

"We used to build tree forts in the woods and go mushroom hunting," said Liz.

"And we had a dog," I said. "We gave him away when we came here."

"I'm sure you miss him," said Mrs. Janeski. "You know what I miss? I miss my flower garden. I miss digging my fingers deep down in the soil. I miss my cats. And I miss the sounds of the bullfrogs and the crickets at night. You just can't hear them with all these city noises."

"At least we have ducks and geese here," said Liz.

"Yes, Liz, you're right. I was just thanking the Lord for this pond. It's like a little piece of home."

I said, "Did you get a new job too?"

Mrs. Janeski's eyes looked all wet and shiny. "No," she said. "My husband died a few months ago. My son lives here, and he wanted me to sell the farm and move here closer to his family." She took a deep breath and smiled at us. "He's right, I'm sure. This is the best thing for us all."

Liz reached out and took the lady's hand. "We're glad you moved here, Mrs. Janes— Janes—"

"Why don't you call me Grandma Jan?" said Mrs. Janeski. She pulled Liz close for a sideways hug.

I felt a little left out, so I spoke up. "I just finished first grade," I said. "I can read books with chapters."

Grandma Jan smiled at me. I was glad to see that her eyes looked dry now. I hate it when grandmas cry. "That's wonderful, Micah," she said. "Reading is a lifelong joy. I still treasure some of the books I read when I was your age."

That reminded me of something. "We've been looking for buried treasure here," I said. "We think pirates hid it a long time ago."

"Pirates? Really?" Grandma Jan asked.

"Yeah. Liz thinks they might have buried the gold and jewels somewhere around here."

"Well, if I find any pirate treasure, I'll be sure to let you know," said Grandma Jan.

Liz looked at me as if she thought I was saying too much. I changed the subject a little.

"We thought you were a pirate at first," I said.

"Micah!" said Liz.

Grandma Jan tipped her head back and laughed. "A pirate!"

She got out the white tissue and dabbed at her eyes again. But I don't think she was sad because her smile stayed. "Oh, Micah, I don't think *pirate* is quite the right word for me. Maybe . . . *pilgrim*."

"You mean the Pilgrims we learned about at Thanksgiving?" I asked.

Liz giggled. "You don't really look like a Pilgrim lady. They all wore long black dresses and funny white hats."

"What is a pilgrim?" I asked.

Grandma Jan looked out across the water again. "That's a hard question, Micah. A pilgrim is . . . well, I guess you could say that a pilgrim is anybody who's looking for home."

"We're looking for a house," said Liz. "I guess that makes us pilgrims too. We can all be pilgrims together!"

Grandma Jan winked. "I would like that much better than being a pirate," she said.

Chapter 3

Roses and Thorns

"Micah," said Liz. "We've got to help Grandma Jan."

We were sitting in the kitchen trying to finish our asparagus. Mom had told us not to leave the supper table until we'd eaten every last bit of it. She had just left to take the dirty clothes to the laundry room. Dad was back in the bedroom at the computer.

"How?" I asked.

"We have to help her feel at home here," said Liz. "She really misses her farm. Did you see? She was crying."

I waited till Liz was taking a drink of milk. Then I took a big bite of asparagus and made my best yucky-food face.

She started giggling and spit out her milk. Then she hiccupped. We both laughed so hard we snorted.

"Micah!" she said when she could talk again. "Stop! I'm being serious." She leaned forward. "I have an idea."

I stopped laughing. I had to hear this. Liz's ideas were always good.

"You know how Grandma Jan said the pond was a little piece of home? Well, we have to find more little pieces of home to give her. She can put them all together. And then she'll really feel like this is her home."

"Where can we find pieces of home?" I asked.

"Just stuff that reminds her of her farm. I've got one idea already." Her voice dropped to a whisper. "The rosebush."

I speared another bite of asparagus with my fork. "What rosebush?" I asked out loud.

"Shh!" Liz glanced toward the bedroom. "We have to keep this a secret. There's a rosebush growing outside our back door, right by the sandbox. Haven't you seen it?"

"Oh. Yeah." I remembered now. I had poked my finger on a thorn when I tried to smell a rose.

"Remember how Grandma Jan said she misses her flowers? We'll move our rosebush and plant it outside her back door," said Liz. "Then she'll always have flowers."

"We don't know which door is hers," I said.

"She told us she lives in Apartment 73," said Liz. "All the numbers are on the doors. We'll just find that door and plant the rosebush outside."

"Yeah!" It was a great idea. I stuffed the last three bites of asparagus into my mouth. Liz still had about seven bites left on her plate. I pointed to them. "Hurry up," I said with my mouth full.

She picked up a piece with her fingers and dropped it into her mouth. We both made our best yucky-food faces.

By the time we got outside to dig up the rosebush, it was almost bedtime. "We've got to hurry," said Liz. She fished her shovel out of the sandbox.

"Oh, no!" I yelled.

"Shh! What's wrong, Micah?"

I tried to whisper then, but my voice came out only a half-whisper. "I forgot I broke my shovel. What can I use?"

Liz thought for a minute. "I'll get Mom's garden trowel," she said. "She keeps it under the sink. Wait here."

Mom's garden trowel worked much better than Liz's toy shovel. We took turns using it to dig around the bush. Dirt flew all over the place.

"We've got to make sure we dig up all the roots," whispered Liz. "Plants have to have their roots if you're going to move them."

"How are we going to carry it?" I asked.

"We'll just hold it between us," said Liz. She wiggled the bush. "It's getting looser. We'll be done soon."

I took another turn digging. I grunted and pushed the trowel deep into the ground. Two big clods of dirt broke loose. I grabbed the bush with both hands to wiggle it. But I had forgotten all about the thorns. "Owwww!" I yelled.

"Micah!" Liz clapped her hand over my mouth.

Too late. Dad poked his head out the back door. "What's going on out here?" he asked.

Chapter 4
Frogs and Crickets

Dad and Liz put all the dirt back around the rosebush while Mom put Band-Aids on my fingers. Then we all sat down in the living room for a talk.

"We're renting this apartment," said Dad. "Do you kids understand what that means?"

"It means we're paying to live here," said Liz very quietly.

"That's right. It means that this is not really our home. The house in Michigan was ours. But this apartment isn't. The pond, the trees, the geese, the ducks, the plants, the flowers—none of them are ours. They belong to the apartments. We're just paying to use them for a while."

I sneaked a peek at Liz. I hoped she wouldn't cry. Liz almost always cries when we get in trouble.

"Sorry, Dad," she said. She sniffed and looked down at her lap.

"Sorry, Dad," I added.

"I think it's nice that you wanted to help Grandma Jan," said Mom. "But Apartment 73 is on the third floor. You couldn't have planted the rosebush by her door anyway. Why don't you just go pay her a visit tomorrow? We'll make cookies, and you can take her some."

Liz and I looked at each other. Cookies were nice. But they just weren't the same as a rosebush. Cookies wouldn't remind Grandma Jan of home.

Just before bed, I went into Liz's room. She wasn't playing or reading or anything. She was leaning on her windowsill, staring out at the dark.

"Don't feel bad, Liz," I said. "At least we didn't get in very much trouble."

Liz turned away from her window, all happy and sparkly-looking. "I have another idea, Micah," she said.

"What is it?" I climbed up on her bed and sat down.

"I was looking out at the pond in the dark," said Liz. "And I thought of another little piece of home that Grandma Jan misses."

"What?"

"Frogs and crickets!" Liz pulled her knees up and sat hugging them. "Remember how she said she used to hear the frogs and crickets at night? But now she can't hear them because of the city noise."

"Yeah, I remember."

"Well, we'll catch some frogs and crickets and take them to her! She can keep them in a jar by her bed and hear them at night."

"Good idea!" I bounced up and down on the bed. "Let's do it tomorrow."

Mom used up the last of the oatmeal making cookies the next day.

"Can we have that oatmeal container for bug catching?" asked Liz.

Oatmeal containers are great for bugs. They don't need to be rinsed out. Their lids are soft and easy to punch holes in. And they're big, so they hold a lot.

"Sure," said Mom. "Why don't you go catch some bugs while I get these cookies in the oven?"

We didn't tell her why we wanted the bugs, and she didn't ask us. We used to catch bugs all the time in Michigan. No big deal.

We filled the container about half-full with grass and leaves and sticks. That would make the bugs feel at home. Frogs might need water, though. So we sprinkled some pond water over the top of everything. Just a little bit—not enough to soak through.

Catching frogs and crickets took longer than we thought it would. We took a snack break when the cookies came out of the oven. Then we went at it again.

I finally plopped down in the grass near the pond. The sun was high in the sky. We had a couple of crickets, but we still hadn't found any frogs.

"Maybe the ducks and geese eat them all," said Liz. "Maybe that's why we can't find very many."

And right then I saw one. "A frog!" I shouted.

It was on a rock by the water. I crouched down and slowly moved closer and closer. The frog didn't move. I stretched my hands out toward it. Slowly, slowly, slowly . . .

And then I pounced! But I didn't just pounce. I lost my balance. The next thing I felt was cold water splashing all over me as I tumbled headfirst into the pond. I made sure I held onto that frog though. I wasn't going to lose him after all that!

Chapter 5

The Trouble with Oatmeal Containers

By lunchtime, we had two frogs and four crickets. Liz had caught the other frog up closer to the apartment. Once I got cleaned up and into dry clothes, Mom told us we had to stay away from the pond the rest of the day.

But that was all right. We were going to Grandma Jan's anyway.

We set out right after lunch with a tin of cookies and our oatmeal container. This time we were sure our plan would work. I could imagine Grandma Jan's face lighting up when she saw the little piece of home we were bringing.

We found Grandma Jan's door, Number 73, on the third floor. Voices came from inside. "She has company," said Liz. "Maybe we should just leave the stuff outside the door."

But I really wanted to see Grandma Jan. "We can just stay a minute," I said.

"Okay." Liz knocked on the door.

Grandma Jan seemed glad to see us. "Come in, Liz and Micah," she said. "I'd like you to meet my granddaughters. We've just finished lunch."

Two teenage girls were sitting at Grandma Jan's table. "This is Brianne, and this is Emily. Girls, these are my new friends Liz and Micah."

"Hi," we all said.

"Why don't we sit down in the living room," said Grandma Jan.

Liz and I sat down on the puffy blue couch. There was a coffee table in front of the couch with books and magazines on it. I looked around the room. There was only one picture on the wall. I could see a lot of green in it, but I couldn't tell what it was.

I pointed to it. "What is that a picture of?"

Grandma Jan walked over and stood in front of the picture. "This is a photograph of our farm," she said. "A pilot took the picture from the air." She pointed to something in one corner near the frame. "This is our house," she said. "We had a big front porch with a swing on it. And we always kept the two porch lights shining at night. I can remember driving up this road late in the evening, coming home.

There's nothing quite like seeing the home lights shining out across the quiet fields."

For a moment the room was all still like some kind of spell had fallen on us. Then Emily broke it with a big yawn. "Grandma, can we watch TV?" she asked.

Grandma Jan turned her eyes away from the picture and looked at Emily. Her face looked sad like it had yesterday. "Not while we have guests here, Emily," she said.

"Oh, we're not staying long," Liz said quickly. "We just came to bring you something." She picked up the tin of cookies. "Our mom made these for you this morning."

"Well, how kind of her! Please tell your mother I said thank you." Grandma Jan lifted the lid of the tin and peeked inside. "Shall we have some now?"

Liz and I had just had some for our lunch. We looked at each other and shrugged. "Sure," we said.

Grandma Jan went into the kitchen to get some plates. I looked down at the oatmeal container in my hands. I could hardly wait to tell her what else we'd brought. I knew this would cheer her up.

She came back and set the cookies out on the coffee table.

"We brought you something else too," I said. I held up the oatmeal container. But the trouble with oatmeal containers is that you can't show anybody what's inside them unless you take off their lids. I carried it over to Grandma Jan's chair and opened the lid just a crack. "Look inside," I said.

She couldn't see anything. I took the lid completely off. "Now can you see?" I asked.

Plop! One of the frogs sprang out of the container and landed on the coffee table. I've never seen two teenage girls jump up so fast in my life. Emily screamed and ran for the kitchen. Brianne followed her, shouting, "What is it? What is it?"

"It's just a little frog," I said.

"Micah, catch it! Put it back!" Liz was yelling.

I dived for the frog. But right about then, I saw something black hopping over by the couch. A cricket was loose too!

Chapter 6
The Perfect House

"Grandma!" Brianne cried. She was standing up on a kitchen chair hiding her face in her hands. "Make them kill those things!"

"Oooh! Oooh!" Emily squealed. "Look how high it can hop!"

It was so loud and screamy in that room I could hardly think. I squished the frog into my pocket and then pounced on the cricket. I ran back to Grandma Jan's chair. She opened the lid of the container again, just a crack, and I dumped the creatures inside.

"We're so sorry, Grandma Jan," Liz was saying. "We just wanted to help you—"

Grandma Jan spoke calmly. "Girls, get ahold of yourselves. Get down from those chairs. Micah has caught the critters now. Everything is safe."

"We'd better go now," said Liz. She grabbed my hand and walked quickly to the door.

"Thank you, Liz and Micah," said Grandma Jan.

I looked back over my shoulder at her. She was holding the oatmeal container close in her arms. And she was smiling again now. Her eyes looked all crinkly and happy. "Please come again, you two—soon. This old place needs the excitement."

Liz scolded me all the way home. "Micah, you shouldn't have taken the lid all the way off," she said. "You should've known they'd get out! Brianne and Emily probably hate us now."

"I don't care," I said. I didn't think much of Brianne and Emily either. I sure was glad Liz wasn't screamy like they were about bugs and frogs.

"But if we scare the girls away, they'll never come to see Grandma Jan anymore," said Liz.

"Oh." I thought about that for a while. I didn't want Grandma Jan to be lonely.

"We've got to think of a better idea," said Liz. "One that won't cause any trouble for anybody."

We spent the afternoon inside since we couldn't go out by the pond. We sat at the table and drew treasure maps. I made mine look like

the picture of Grandma Jan's farm. I drew the
two porch lights shining. I drew a big red *X* out
in one of the fields.

"How would you all like to go look at a house
tonight?" asked Dad at supper.

"Where is it?" Liz asked.

"It's here in this neighborhood," said Dad.
"It's on Ashdale Street. It's got a big yard. And
three bedrooms. You kids could have your own
rooms."

That sounded great to me. Right now I was
sleeping on a bed that pulled out of the couch
in the living room. It was a fun place to sleep.
But my own room, like I'd had in Michigan,
might be even better.

We drove over to Ashdale Street after
supper. The house was gray with a black door.
I went upstairs to look at the room that might

be mine. The roof sloped on one side. I would want my bed under the sloping part, right by the window.

I looked out the window at the backyard. It was big. It didn't have a pond, of course. But it had lots of trees. Maybe we could put up a tire swing.

Miss Reeves, the lady who was helping us find a house, was there. Mom and Dad talked to her till it started to get dark. Liz and I mostly spent the time trying to catch fireflies. I caught a great big one. Its light was so bright that it could have been a flashlight.

"It would be the perfect house for us," Mom said to Dad on the way home.

I opened my cupped hands to peek at my firefly. He didn't seem to want to light up anymore. Maybe he was sad that I had taken him away from his home.

I thought about the pond and the buried treasure and the frogs and Grandma Jan and even those pesky geese and my pullout bed. All of a sudden, I wasn't so sure I wanted that perfect house.

Chapter 7

In the Window Well

Not long after that we had a rainy day. It rained until evening. When it stopped, Liz and I went out to the front parking lot to wade in the puddles.

The parking lot is on a hill. When it rains, water runs down like a stream to the lowest part. Liz and I like to have races through the stream. It kind of reminds us of our creek back home in Michigan.

We had just finished racing to the bottom of the hill. I won. I was heading back up to the top when Liz said, "Wait! Listen."

I heard it too then. It was a tiny little cry. It sounded like an animal in trouble.

Liz mimicked the cry. "Where are you?" she called softly.

The cry kept coming. We moved toward it. At last we tracked the sound to a window well beside a basement window. We looked down into it. A small gray kitten was huddled in one corner. His fur was wet and his eyes were turned up to us.

"Oh, look," said Liz. "He's scared. I think he must have fallen in here, and now he's stuck."

"I wonder whose kitten he is," I said.

"I know he doesn't belong to anybody in these apartments," said Liz. "We're not allowed to have pets."

"He's probably hungry," I said.

Liz leaned over and picked up the kitten. His cries stopped. He snuggled against Liz's shirt. "Poor little kitty," she said. "Let me see if I can dry you off a little."

"What are we going to do with him?" I asked Liz.

Liz looked at me with her eyes all lit up. It's the look she gets when she has an idea. "I've got it!" she said. "We can give the kitten to Grandma Jan! Remember? She said she had cats on her farm. It will remind her of home."

I frowned. "But she lives in these apartments too," I said. "So she can't have pets."

"Maybe it will be okay because she's old and lonely," said Liz. "We can talk to Mrs. Melzer about it." Mrs. Melzer was the lady in charge of the apartments.

The kitten purred and swished his tail against Liz's chin. "We need to do something with him right now," she said. "Let's take him to Grandma Jan. She'll know what to do."

"Can I hold him?"

Liz handed me the kitten, and I held him against me as we walked to Grandma Jan's apartment.

Grandma Jan answered our knock with a big smile. "Come in, Liz and Micah!" she said. "Oh, and who is this that you've brought with you?"

"We found him just now," said Liz. "Outside in the window well. He's wet and cold and hungry, and we thought you might want to keep him."

I moved closer so Grandma Jan could pet the kitten.

"Well, now I don't know about keeping him," she said. "There are rules about that. But you're right—he is cold and hungry. Why don't we get you something to eat, little fella?"

"He probably wants some milk," said Liz.

We followed Grandma Jan into her kitchen. She opened her cupboard. "Do you know what I have?" she asked. "Some kitty formula from my days on the farm." She laughed. "I can't believe I kept it. But I found it when I was packing and just couldn't bring myself to throw it out. I learned how to make it myself." She pulled a jar off a high shelf. "This would be as close to his mama's milk as we could get. Let's try feeding him with an eyedropper."

Grandma Jan mixed the formula and filled the eyedropper. She sat down in a kitchen chair with the kitten in her lap. She pushed the end of the dropper into the kitten's mouth. Kind of the way you would give a baby its bottle. "I used to do this at home on my farm," she said. "We had one mama cat who died right after having a litter of kittens. Poor little things. But we took care of them, and they all turned out nice and healthy."

"We knew you would know just what to do," said Liz. "That's why we brought him to you. We thought he might make you less lonely for the country. The kitten would be a little piece of home—you know, like the pond."

"And the frogs and crickets," I said. "And the rosebush."

"Micah!" said Liz. I put my hand over my mouth. I forgot that we'd never told Grandma Jan about the rosebush.

Grandma Jan just smiled. "Well, if there weren't a no-pets rule, I could get used to having a kitten around the place. I could get used to that really fast."

Chapter 8
Saying Goodbye

Liz reached out and touched the kitten. "He's still kind of wet, isn't he?"

"Yes," said Grandma Jan. "Let's dry him off a little. Liz, could you get a clean towel from the closet in the hall, please?"

Liz came back with a soft blue towel. The kitten was still drinking. He batted his little paw at the eyedropper.

"There, now, little fella, I think you've had enough for one meal," said Grandma Jan. She wrapped the kitten up in the towel so that even his head was covered. He mewed and poked his head out. We laughed.

"I've noticed a stray cat running around here," Grandma Jan said. "I guess she had kittens. This one must have gotten lost."

"I'm sure Mrs. Melzer would let you keep him, Grandma Jan," I said.

"Yeah," said Liz. "Maybe if we talked to her . . ."

"Let's call her right now," said Grandma Jan. "I don't think she'll let me keep him. But she can tell us what we need to do with him."

Grandma Jan handed the kitten to me and picked up the phone. He climbed up onto my shoulder. I could feel his little claws gripping my shirt.

"We need to give him a name," said Liz.

The kitten's tail tickled my chin. I laughed. "We could call him Tickler."

Liz frowned and watched the kitten, deep in thought. "What about Pilgrim?" she said.

"Pilgrim?"

"Grandma Jan said a pilgrim is someone who's looking for a home. This kitten needs a home."

I giggled as the kitten climbed back down my shirt. "I like that name," I said. "Pilgrim, that tickles!"

"Thank you, Mrs. Melzer," Grandma Jan was saying. "Yes, I know. We'll see what we can do." She hung up the phone.

"What did she say?" Liz asked.

"She said it's supposed to rain some more tonight, so she'll let me keep the kitten here. Just for tonight. But if we don't find a home for him tomorrow, she'll take him to the Humane Society."

"His name is Pilgrim," I told her.

"Pilgrim? Well, you'll fit right in with us, little fella. Don't worry—we'll try to find you a home."

"Do you think Brianne and Emily would want him?" Liz asked.

"Now that's a thought," said Grandma Jan. She looked at her watch. "It's getting late now. I'll call them first thing tomorrow. You kids better be running along. Your parents will be wondering where you are."

Liz gave Pilgrim a goodbye kiss, and I shook his paw. "We'll come back and see you tomorrow," said Liz as we left.

I was a little afraid Mom would be upset with us for coming home late. "We were at Grandma Jan's," I said as soon as we came in the back door.

But Mom was not upset. She was in the kitchen getting out ice cream bowls. "Liz! Micah!" she said. Her eyes were all sparkly like Liz's when she had an idea. "Come in and sit down. Dad has some news to tell you."

Dad was already sitting at the table. "I just got off the phone with Miss Reeves," he said. "We have a new house!"

"The gray one on Ashdale?" asked Liz.

"That's the one," said Dad. "I made an offer the other day, and Miss Reeves just called and said the owner wants to sell it to us. So we'll be moving soon!"

"Yippee!" said Liz.

"Let's have ice cream to celebrate!" said Mom.

I was quiet. I didn't turn down the ice cream, of course. But I thought about saying goodbye to the pond. And to Pilgrim. And to Grandma Jan.

Chapter 9
Out of Ideas

"We're moving," I said to Grandma Jan. I said it as soon as she answered our knock the next morning. No use waiting to tell her. She'd find out soon enough anyway.

Her smile faded. "Moving? When? Where?"

"We found a house," said Liz. "It's in this neighborhood. On Ashdale Street."

Grandma Jan's smile came back. "Well, that's wonderful!" she said. "I'm glad you're not going far away. You can still come visit me."

I hadn't thought about that. That was true. And when we came to visit Grandma Jan, we could play at the pond. Maybe we could even hunt some more for the buried treasure.

But we'd never see Pilgrim again after he went to live with Brianne and Emily. Poor Pilgrim. He'd probably hate living with those screamy girls.

"How's Pilgrim?" I asked.

"Oh, he's doing fine," said Grandma Jan. "Acting like he owns the place already."

She held her finger up to her lips. "He's found himself a bed," she said. "Come see where he's sleeping."

We found the kitten in Grandma Jan's sewing basket. He was all snuggled up with the scraps of green wool fabric in there.

"Oh, he looks cute," said Liz. "I wish you could keep him, Grandma Jan."

"Well," said Grandma Jan, "I have an idea. Brianne and Emily can't take him at their house. Their mother is allergic to cats. I'd forgotten about that. But, since you two will be moving to a house soon . . ." She stopped and raised her eyebrows at us.

Liz looked at me. "We could take Pilgrim!" she cried. She started jumping up and down. "Why didn't we think of that last night, Micah? I know Mom and Dad will let us. They let us have a dog in Michigan. They have to let us."

"But what will we do with him until then?" I asked. "Mrs. Melzer said we had to find him a home today."

"I'll have another talk with Mrs. Melzer," said Grandma Jan. "She might allow me to keep him a little longer if a home has been promised to him soon. And I could give him the care he needs with my kitty formula."

Liz leaned over and whispered in the kitten's ear. "Pilgrim, I think we've found you a home."

Pilgrim's ear twitched. But he went right on sleeping.

We talked to Mom and Dad, and Grandma Jan talked to Mrs. Melzer. They all said they'd think about it. So that night, Liz and I knelt beside her bed and prayed. We prayed really hard. And the next day—everybody said yes!

We spent a lot of time helping Mom pack boxes. A lot of our stuff was already in boxes down in the basement of the apartment building. But we had to pack up the stuff we'd been using. Packing isn't very much fun. But it made me excited to move into our new house.

Liz and I went to visit Pilgrim and Grandma Jan every day. Pilgrim was turning out to be a lot fluffier and cuter than he'd been at first. Grandma Jan gave us tips about caring for him. She really knew what she was doing!

Liz and I tried a few more times to find the pirate treasure. One day while we were digging

in a muddy place near the pond, Liz said, "Micah, I've been thinking."

"Thinking about what?"

"We never found a little piece of home for Grandma Jan to keep. I mean, she's getting to keep Pilgrim for a few weeks. But then she has to give him back to us."

"What about the frogs and crickets?" I asked.

Liz shook her head. "I don't think that was a very good idea. If she kept them at all, I don't think she keeps them inside. I've never seen them in her apartment anywhere."

"Well, at least we tried," I said.

"I can't think of any more ideas," said Liz.

I stopped digging and looked at her. I could never, ever remember a time when Liz had been out of ideas.

"Can you think of anything?" she asked.

I looked around at the geese, the ducks, the trees, the pond, the bushes, and the flowers. Nothing was ours to give away.

"No," I said.

Chapter 10
Home Lights Shining

It was the evening before moving day. I'd been helping Dad carry boxes out to our car.

"Hello, Micah!" someone called to me.

It was Grandma Jan. She had a garden trowel just like Mom's. She was on her hands and knees digging in the dirt along the curb.

"Grandma Jan, what are you doing?" I asked.

"I'm getting ready to plant some flowers," she said. Her smile looked brighter than I'd ever seen it. "Mrs. Melzer asked me to help make things prettier around here. I told her I'd love to."

Sitting beside her were little black cartons with flowers in them. "Are those the ones you're going to plant?" I asked.

"Yes. A few pansies along this curb would brighten up the parking lot, don't you think?"

"Sure," I said. Then I added, "At first I thought you were digging for treasure."

She tipped her head back and laughed. "Oh, no, Micah," she said. Then she stopped laughing, but her smile stayed. "No, I think I've already found my treasure."

"You have?" I wanted to hear about this.

Grandma Jan laid down her spade and sat back on her heels. "Pirate treasure is one kind of treasure, Micah. But there are other kinds."

"Like what?" I came over and sat down on the curb next to her.

She picked up one of the pansies and set it in a hole she had dug. Then she carefully patted dirt all around it. She handed me another pansy, and I did the same thing. But mine was

kind of leaning over when I got done with it. Grandma Jan lifted it up straight and packed the dirt tighter around it. Then it stood tall.

"Well, Micah," she said finally, "the Lord has been showing me that there's treasure all around me here. The kind of treasure that lasts forever."

She stopped talking for a minute and ran her fingers through the dirt.

"What kind of treasure lasts forever?" I asked. I reached for another pansy.

"People," said Grandma Jan. "I have a lot of treasures right here where I am. Brianne and Emily need me. And Mrs. Melzer and I have become friends. She lost her husband too, a few years ago. She's lonely, Micah. I think she needs someone to talk to once in a while."

She set another pansy in its hole. She leaned back to make sure it was lined up with the others.

"And then I have a little boy and girl named Liz and Micah who bring me joy," she said. She looked over at me and her eyes were all wet and shiny. "They bring me joy because of their kind, loving hearts. And you know, Micah, any place where you have that kind of treasure is home."

I looked down at the flower I was working on. I sure hoped Grandma Jan wouldn't start crying. I didn't even have any tissues.

But then she laughed a little. "I think Pilgrim's about ready for moving day," she said. "He's been all cooped up in my little place too long. He needs a home of his own. A home with a yard and lots of space to play in."

I frowned. "I guess Pilgrim isn't really a pilgrim anymore," I said. "Because he's found a home."

"He's found a home, all right—and so have you," said Grandma Jan.

"Yeah." I looked up at her and said, "And I guess you have too."

"I guess I have."

Grandma Jan patted the dirt around the last pansy. We were both really quiet for a minute, looking at the pretty little row of flowers. Then Grandma Jan said in a whisper, "Do you hear them?"

"Hear what?"

"Crickets!"

I listened. Sure enough. It was quiet enough to hear the soft *chirp-chirp* of the crickets tonight.

Grandma Jan grabbed her spade and her empty flower carton and stood up. "It's getting dark. Ready to go in now?" She held out her hand to me.

I took her hand, and she pulled me up. Just as we turned back to the apartments, the lights beside each door all clicked on at once. I knew they all came on at a certain time, but I'd never seen them do it before. It looked like dozens of little porch lights.

I pointed. "Look, Grandma Jan! The home lights are shining!"

She squeezed my hand. "Yes, Micah," she said, "they certainly are."